POKÉMON

DIAMOND AND PEARL

COAL BADGE BATTLE

Based on "O'er the Rampardos We Watched!"

ADAPTED BY
TRACEY WEST

SCHOLASTIC INC.

New York   Toronto   London   Auckland   Sydney
Mexico City   New Delhi   Hong Kong   Buenos Aires

ISBN-13: 978-0-545-01414-4
ISBN-10: 0-545-01414-X

Published by Scholastic Inc.
SCHOLASTIC and associated logos are trademarks and/or registered trademarks of Scholastic Inc.

12 11 10 9 8 7 6 5 4 3 2 1   8 9 10 11 12/0

Cover Designed by Henry Ng
Interior Designed by Kay Petronio

Printed in the U.S.A.
First printing, March 2008

Ash Ketchum stood on the rocky
field of the Oreburgh City Gym.
He faced Roark, the Gym Leader.
"I'm leaving here with a Gym
Badge for sure!" Ash said.

Brock sat in the stands with his Sudowoodo and Croagunk.

Dawn cheered Ash with her Buneary and Piplup.

"Go, Ash, number one! Do it right and have some fun!"

Ash was ready for this Gym battle.

Roark had a new Rampardos. But Ash had trained very hard to beat it.

The battle began.

"Onix, let's go!" Roark cried.

"Pikachu, I choose you!" Ash said.

"Pikachu, Quick Attack!" Ash yelled.

Pikachu ran at the big Rock-type Pokémon. Onix tried to use Slam. But Pikachu climbed up Onix's long neck.

"Onix, use Screech!" Roark yelled.

Onix let out a loud roar. Pikachu held on tightly. Then Ash told Pikachu to use Iron Tail.

Pikachu jumped up. White light shone from Pikachu's tail. *Bam!* The tail smacked Onix.

"Quick, Onix," Roark said. "Use Double Edge!"

Onix's body glowed as it got ready for the strong attack. But Ash had a new move to try.

"Spin, Pikachu!" Ash cried.

Pikachu jumped and spun at the same time. It dodged the attack!

"Now finish it with Iron Tail!"
Ash said.

But Onix used Slam. It hit
Pikachu with its heavy tail.

Pikachu smashed into a pile of
rocks!

"*Pikachuuuuuu!*" The Electric-type Pokémon used Thunderbolt. Pikachu blasted out of the rock pile. It used Iron Tail on Onix again. The big Pokémon fainted!

Ash had won the first round. But the battle wasn't over yet.

"Geodude, let's go!" Roark cried.

"Pikachu, you take a break," Ash said.

Ash threw out a Poké Ball.
"All right," he said. "Aipom, I choose you!"

Geodude rolled across the field to attack Aipom.

Aipom used Double Team. A bunch of fake Aipom appeared. Geodude didn't know which one to attack! It missed.

"Aipom, Focus Punch!" Ash cried.
Aipom tried to punch Geodude.
But the Rock-and-Ground-type
Pokémon blocked it.

Then Geodude used Rollout
again. This time, Aipom dodged the
move by spinning.

"All right, Aipom. Focus Punch!"
Ash yelled.

Slam! Aipom used the hand on
the end of its tail to deliver the
punch.

Geodude fainted!

"That's two wins in a row!"
Dawn cheered.

"But don't forget about Roark's last Pokémon," Brock said. He knew Roark was saving his best Pokémon for last.

"Go, Rampardos!" Roark
yelled.

The tough Rock-type Pokémon
came out. Rampardos had a head
as hard as iron. Its Headbutt
could take down a tall tree.

"Here we go," Ash said. "Time to get busy!"

Aipom used Swift. Stars flew across the field at Rampardos. But the big Pokémon did not even move.

"Oh man," Ash moaned. "How am I going to get past Rampardos's defense?"

"Now it's our turn," Roark said. "Rampardos, Headbutt!"

Bam! Rampardos slammed into the little Pokémon with its hard head.

Aipom fainted! Ash sent in Pikachu next.

Pikachu started off with a Thunderbolt. Rampardos dodged it.

Then Rampardos used Zen Headbutt. Pikachu tried to dodge the powerful attack.

But Rampardos was too fast. Roark had trained it well.

Rampardos aimed another Headbutt at Pikachu.

"Jump, Pikachu!" Ash yelled.

Pikachu jumped into another amazing spin. But Rampardos quickly bashed Pikachu with another Zen Headbutt.

Pikachu fainted!

Ash ran to Pikachu.

"Are you okay?" he asked.

Pikachu nodded.

In the stands, Brock frowned.

"Now Turtwig's the only one left."

The little Grass-type Pokémon
came out of its Poké Ball.
Ash knew Turtwig was tougher
than it looked. But was it tough
enough to take down Rampardos?

The last round of the battle began.

Turtwig and Rampardos ran across the field.

Turtwig dodged a Headbutt. Then, *chomp*! It used Bite on Rampardos's tail.

The big Pokémon went flying into a pile of dirt!

"Razor Leaf, go!" Ash yelled.
Turtwig sent sharp leaves flying
at Rampardos. But Rampardos
used Flamethrower. It burned all
the leaves!

"No good," Ash said. "We're too
far away for Razor Leaf to work."

"Use Head Smash, Rampardos, now!" Roark cried.

Rampardos charged across the field. Its body glowed with super strength.

Bam! Rampardos smashed into Turtwig. The little Pokémon flew up. Then it landed in the dirt.

Turtwig used Synthesis to get energy from the sun.

Rampardos used Flamethrower again.

Turtwig jumped over the hot flames.

Ash had to find a way to get Turtwig close to Rampardos without getting hit by Flamethrower.

"That's it!" Ash cried. "Turtwig, use Razor Leaf while you run!"

Turtwig obeyed. The flying leaves hid Turtwig. Rampardos couldn't aim an attack!

Rampardos charged at Turtwig.

"Jump!" Ash yelled.

"Still trying to get behind us?" Roark asked. "Rampardos, use Jump, too!"

Both Pokémon jumped. Then
Turtwig made a surprise move.
It rolled right underneath
Rampardos!

Turtwig blasted Rampardos with Razor Leaf. The big Pokémon had no defense against the surprise attack. Rampardos fainted!

"Turtwig, we did it!" Ash cheered. They won the Gym battle!

"Here's proof of your Oreburgh Gym victory," Roark said. "The Coal Badge."

Ash picked up the shiny metal badge.

"We just got a Coal Badge!" he cried. It felt great to win.

But he couldn't have done it without his Pokémon!